c. 1

398
PHI   Philip, Neil
       Drakestail visits the
       king.

DATE DUE		
DEC 7 '88	Norma	
DEC 13 '88	Roland	
Jan 4 '89	Patricia	
JAN 18 '89	Jonathan	
JAN 25 '89	Marcel	
FEB 22 '89	Marcel	
MAR 8 '89	Matt	
MAY 31 '89	Pamerah	

DRAKESTAIL
Visits the King

A Magic Lantern Fairy Tale

Retold by Neil Philip

Illustrated by Henry Underhill

Philomel Books
New York

For Jessica

It was a time of suspense, waiting and incredible excitement, those wonderful nights when the family gathered on the floor and in armchairs around the Magic Lantern to watch fairies and giants and generals perform for them in a circle of light on their very wall. Grandfather of the film projector, the Magic Lantern was first shown in Rome in 1646, but it came into its own in what is called the Golden Age of Toys when it became the darling of Victorian families. Brilliantly painted colored slides charmed Grandma and Uncle Harry as well as three-year-old Tess and ten-year-old John. Christmas, birthdays – no occasion was too large or too small to bring out the Magic Lantern. That Henry Underhill's original slides have been discovered and used to illustrate the wonderful French tale, *Drakestail*, revives this delight from the past for the enchantment of a new generation of children. *And now, the lantern is lit. The beam of light is aimed at the page. Begin.*

Copyright © Text: Neil Philip 1986. Copyright © Illustrations: The Albion Press Ltd 1986. Copyright © Volume: The Albion Press Ltd 1986. First American edition published in 1986 by Philomel Books, a member of The Putnam Publishing Group, 51 Madison Avenue, New York, NY 10010. Printed and bound in Italy. All Rights reserved. Designer: Emma Bradford. L.C. Number 86–9306. ISBN 0–399–21392–9

The Albion Press would like to thank the Folklore Society for its kind permission to reproduce these lantern slides.

DRAKESTAIL was very small, and that's why they called him Drakestail. But little as he was, he had brains and kept his wits about him: he started with nothing, and he ended up with a hundred pounds.

Now the king of the land, who was a spendthrift and never had any money, heard about Drakestail's nest-egg, and one day he went in person to borrow it. My word, Drakestail strutted about a bit after he'd lent his money to the king.

But two years later, seeing as the king hadn't paid anything back, Drakestail began to fret. He decided to go himself to the king and demand his money back.

So one fine morning, here's Drakestail walking along the road all trim and sprightly, singing:

> Quack! Quack!
> Quack! Quack! Quack!
> When shall I get my money back?

He hadn't gone but a hundred steps, when he met Friend Fox doing his rounds.

"Hello, Drakestail," says Friend Fox. "And where are we going so bright and early?"

"I'm going to see the king, to get back what he owes me."

"Oh, take me with you."

Drakestail thought: You can never have too many friends. So he says, "I'd like that. But on all fours you'll soon get tired. Make yourself small, go down my gullet and into my gizzard, and I will carry you."

"What a brain-wave!" says Friend Fox.

Open wide! and he pops down Drakestail's throat like a letter into a letterbox.

Then Drakestail sets off again all trim and sprightly, singing:

Quack! Quack!
Quack! Quack! Quack!
When shall I get my money back?

He hadn't gone but a hundred steps, when he met Lady-friend Ladder, propped against her wall.

"Hello there, my little Drakestail," says she. "Where are you off to so bold?"

"I'm going to see the king, to get back what he owes me."

"Oh, take me with you."

And Drakestail thought: You can never have too many friends. So he says, "I'd like that, but with your wooden legs, you'd soon be tired. Make yourself small, go down my gullet and into my gizzard, and I will carry you."

"Sheer genius!" says Lady-friend Ladder.

Open wide! and she slips down Drakestail's throat to join Friend Fox.

And, Quack! Quack! Quack! Drakestail is back on the road, spruce as ever.

A hundred steps on, he came to his Lady-love River, gently sunning herself.

"It's you, sweetheart," says she. "Where are you going all alone on this rotten road, with your cocked tail?"

"I'm going to see the king, you know, to get back what he owes me."

"Oh, take me with you."

And Drakestail thought: You can never have too many friends. So he says, "I'd like that. But the way you idle along, you'd soon be tired. Make yourself small, go down my gullet and into my gizzard, and I will carry you."

"A brilliant notion!" says Lady-love River.

Open wide! and down she flows *glug, glug, glug* to take her place between Friend Fox and Lady-friend Ladder.

And, Quack! Quack! Quack! Drakestail goes singing down the road.

Just around the corner, who should he meet but General Wasp's Nest, drilling his wasps.

"Hello there, Drakestail!" says General Wasp's Nest. "Where are you off to so trim and sprightly?"

"I'm going to see the king, to get back what he owes me."

"Oh, take me with you."

And Drakestail thought: You can't have too many friends. So he says, "I'd like that. But with your troops to drag along, you'd soon be tired. Make yourself small, go down my gullet and into my gizzard, and I will carry you."

"You're the one for ideas!" says General Wasp's Nest.

And, left! right! he and his army go down the same route as the others. There isn't much room, but by squeezing up a bit they all fit in, and Drakestail sets off again with a swing in his song.

He arrived at last at the capital, and marched straight down the main street, right up to the palace. My! the folk stared and wondered when they heard his song:

Quack! Quack!
Quack! Quack! Quack!
When shall I get my money back?

He raps with the knocker: rat-a-tat-tat!

"Who's there?" asks the maid through the door.

"It's me, Drakestail . . . I want to talk to the king."

"Talk to the king! That's a good one. The king is eating and doesn't want to be disturbed."

"Tell him it's me, and he knows why I'm here."

The maid went to tell the king. He was just sitting down to eat with a napkin tucked into his neck, and all his ministers about him.

"Good! Good!" said the king with a laugh. "I know who that is. Let him in and then put him with the turkeys and the hens."

Back goes the maid. "Just trouble yourself to step inside," she says.

"Oh good!" says Drakestail. "Now I'll see how they eat at court."

"This way, this way," says the maid. "Just one step more . . . that's it . . . you're there!"

"What's this? What's this? In the poultry yard?"
Just think how angry Drakestail was.
"So that's your game!" he says. "You just wait. I'll make you see me." And he set up his song:

> Quack! Quack!
> Quack! Quack! Quack!
> When shall I get my money back?

Now turkeys and hens are animals that hate anyone different from them, and when they saw the newcomer, what sort of a character he was, and heard him singing away, they started looking at him out of the corners of their eyes, and gabbling "What's this? Who's he think he is?" And they set on him in a mob to peck him to death.

I'm in for it! thought Drakestail. But luckily he remembers Friend Fox, and calls out,

> Fox, fox!
> Hurry up!
> Help me now
> Or I'm a dead duck!

Friend Fox was just waiting for the word. He throws himself on those wicked fowls and *quick! quack! snick! snack!* he shows them his fine teeth. In five minutes there isn't one left alive.

And happy Drakestail starts once more to sing:

> Quack! Quack!
> Quack! Quack! Quack!
> When shall I get my money back!

When the king — who was still stuffing himself — heard that little ditty, and when the maid told him about the state of the yard, he threw a fit. "That miserable tail of a drake!" he shouted. "Chuck him in the well and make an end of it."

Drakestail had no hope of getting out of a hole so deep. But he calls out:

> Lady-friend Ladder,
> Lady-friend Ladder,
> Hurry up.
> Come out at once,
> Or I'm a dead duck.

Lady-friend Ladder was just waiting for the word. In two shakes her arms are over the rim of the well. Drakestail climbs nimbly up and hup! he's in the yard, in fine voice.

The king was *still* munching, and laughing at the clever way he'd paid Drakestail out. When he heard that song again — Quack! Quack! — he turned red with anger.

He ordered the oven to be stoked, and that miserable tail of a drake thrown into it. "Let him magic himself out of that!" he says.

The oven was hot enough, but Drakestail wasn't frightened. He trusted his sweetheart, Lady-love River.

> River, River
> Flow out quick!
> Douse the fire,
> Or I'm a dead duck!

Lady-love River gushes out, swoosh!, and drowns the fire, along with all those who are feeding it. Then she goes growling round the palace yard till it is all awash.

And happy Drakestail begins to swim and sing, at the top of his voice:

> Quack! Quack!
> Quack! Quack! Quack!
> Give me my dear money back!

The king was still at the table, feeling very smug. But when he heard Drakestail's new song, and found out what was going on, he was wild, and jumped up, shaking his fists.

"Bring him here, so I can cut his throat!" he shouts. "Bring him quick!"

Two servants race off in search of Drakestail.

At last! thought poor Drakestail, as he climbed the great stairs, he's decided to see me.

Imagine his fright, when he saw the king as red as a turkey-cock and surrounded by his ministers, each with a sword in his hand. He thought, this time it's over. But just in time he remembers he still has one friend, and he shouts with his last breath:

> Wasp's Nest, Wasp's Nest,
> Full of pluck:
> Help me now
> Or I'm a dead duck.

What a turn-about!

Buzz, *Buzz*, bayonet! The brave General Wasp's Nest comes out like the cork from a bottle with all his wasps. They swarm over the angry king and his ministers, stinging them so furiously that they leap pell-mell through the window and break their necks on the pavement below.

So here's Drakestail, all of a dither, alone in the big room, and master of the day. He can't believe it.

For all that, he soon remembered what he was there for and began to search for his dear money. But much good it did him to rummage through the drawers — he didn't find anything. It had all been spent.

Ferreting about from room to room, Drakestail came to the one with the throne in it and sat down on it, to think over his adventure.

Meanwhile, the people had found the dead king and his ministers piled higgledy-piggledy on the pavement. They didn't know what to make of that, so they went into the palace to find out what was going on.

When they got to the throne room, the crowd saw there was already someone on the throne, and they shouted in surprise and joy:

The king is dead!
Long live the king!
Heaven has sent him!
Ring-a-ding-ding.

Nothing can amaze Drakestail now. He bows to the crowd as if he has been born to it.

"Fine sort of king a drakestail'll make," muttered one grumbler. But most of the people said, "Better a canny Drakestail than a wastrel like that one lying on the pavement."

That was that, and they ran to take the crown from the dead king and put it on Drakestail. It was just his size.

That's how Drakestail became king.

"And now," he said, when the ceremony was done, "ladies and gentlemen, let's sup! I'm starving."

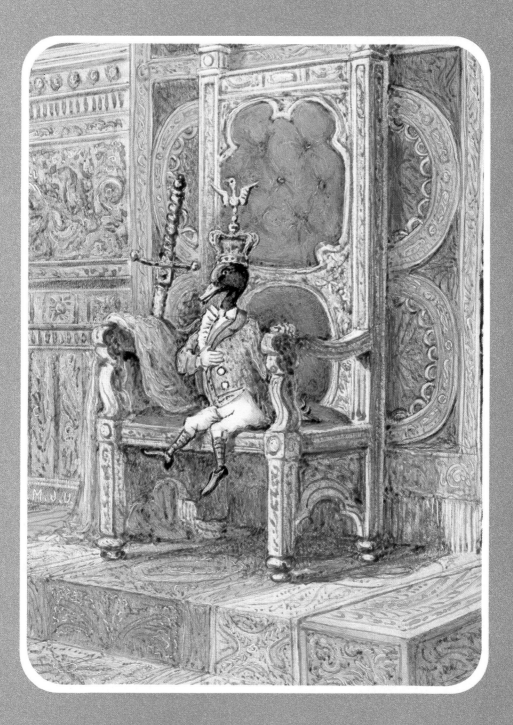